HE WAS MY FRIEND AND A FRIEND TO US ALL. WE WOULDN'T HAVE SURVIVED IF NOT FOR ICHABOD JONES. HE DESERVES BETTER THAN A SHALLOW GRAVE DUG IN THE MIDDLE OF NOWHERE.
Could not have said it better myself.
DID ONE OF YOU JUST SAY SOMETHING?
I did.
SERIOUSLY, THIS ISN'T FUNNY.
I'm not trying to be funny.
STOP IT! THIS IS ANNOYING!
You're starting to look like a crazy person.
WHO ARE YOU?
You have a great purpose. I've been sent to guide you toward it.
THEN WHY HAVEN'T I HEARD YOU BEFORE?

I was helping another, until he met an unfortunate end.

ICHABOD?

Yes.

His purpose was to become a great hero and bring hope back to humanity.

But instead he died saving you.

SO IT'S MY FAULT HE DIED?

ICHABOD JONES

MONSTER HUNTER

VOLUME 2
WELCOME TO MY NIGHTMARE

WRITTEN AND CREATED BY:
RUSSELL NOHELTY

ART AND LETTERS BY:
RENZO PODESTA

STANDARD COVER BY:
RENZO PODESTA

COLOR ASSIST BY:
MARIELA VIGLIETTI

PROOFREAD BY:
KATRINA ROETS

ISBN: 978-1-942350-59-0
© 2019 Russell Nohelty. All rights reserved
First Printing. January 2021.
Printed in China

THIS BOOK IS DEDICATED TO MY WIFE KAREN. WITHOUT HER I WOULD HAVE NEVER BE ABLE TO TAKE ON THE HORRORS OF THE WORLD.

SPECIAL THANKS

Aaron Brower
Alina Schimpf
Amber McNew
Andrew Adams
Andrew Rees
Andrew Smith
Art Spurlock
Arthur Dixon
Bartimaeus
Becky Fuller
Ben Nichols
Bentley Burnham
Beth Culp
Bloodfists
Bob Jacobs
Brandon S Higa
Brett "DJ Archangel" Strassner
Brett Bennett
Brian DiCrocco
Carl W Bishop
Casey
Chris B
Chris Call
Chris Garner
Christopher Prew
Corbineau Alexandre
Daniel Groves
Dave Goldberg
David Chamberlain
David Drummond
David Heald
Daymian Donovan Nycz
Debbie Auld
Dr. Rich Williams
Eddie deAngelini
Emmo Lütringer

Eric Dugal
Eric Müller
Eric Nichols
Erik Sorensen
Faewood
Geoff Weber
GMarkC
Greg Allen
Grubnash
Harley Jebens
J W Lloyd
Jake Schroeder
Jason Sperber
Jeff Lewis
Jennifer Lynn Reynolds
Joanne C. McLaughlin
Jonathan Jaech
Joshua A. Fiser
Kathleen Francis
Kevin
Kimberly and Mark Griffin
Kimberly Herout
Kurt Marquart
Lester Parrott
Lisa Lyons
Lorddragonkin
Marilyn Yasko
Mark Byzewski
Mark Hill
Mathieu Duval
Matthew Carpenter
Maxx Garcia
Melissa Gibbs
Michael Di Salvo
Michael H Bullington

Mika Köykkä
Mitch Rockidge
Monte Hale
Myrddin StarfARI
Myron Fox
Nari A. Muhammad
Neil Moherman
Nicki Matlock
Patrick Hess
Paul Nygard
Paul Trinies
Per Stalby
Philip Hale
Philip M Henderson Jr
Phizbot
Ramsey Church
Rob MacAndrew
Salvator Joseph Tierno Sr.
Samantha
Scott Kilburn
Shalion
Shannon K. Carlin
Shawn Marier
Sophia J Robinson
Stephanie Vincent
Stephen Farbman
Sunyoung Chong
Talinda Willard (everfai)
Tharathip Opaskornkul
The Failed Superheroes Club
Thom "Thom" Verratti
Todd Good
Tofuji
Tymothy
www.gnut.co.uk
Zachary Butler-Jones

Yes. And I'll never forgive you for it.
He was, after all, my dearest friend.
I lied, cheated, and stole the innocence from that boy to assure he was ready to lead the world.
Then he fell for you and it all went to pot.
Now it's your duty to make sure his life wasn't given in vain.
I CAN'T.
I don't believe it either, but then I didn't believe in Ichabod and he wound up being the best human I've ever known.

I'M NO LEADER. I BARELY HELD IT TOGETHER IN THAT BUNKER.
Ichabod was a bus driver and look what he became.
HE BECAME WORM FOOD.
Show some respect! He was a hero.
I'M SORRY.
It's okay. I know you're scared.
WILL I DIE?
If you do, it will be for a greater good. Now grab the knife and address your flock. This will be your totem, the banner behind which you stand.
FRIENDS, I KNOW IT'S BEEN HARD, BUT WE MUST JOURNEY ON. ICHABOD WAS A GREAT MAN. WE WILL HONOR HIM BY THRIVING IN THIS HARSH CLIMATE. TOGETHER WE WILL CREATE A NEW LIFE FOR OURSELVES. IT SHALL BE A UTOPIA!
That kinda sounded like a leader. We'll work on it.

BLINK!
WHAT A WEIRD DREAM.
=YAWN=
CLICK!
A BIZARRE AND HORRIFYING STORY UNFOLDED YESTERDAY AT A LOCAL MENTAL ASYLUM.
AFTER KILLING TWO GUARDS, A MANIAC HELD HIS FELLOW INMATES HOSTAGE.
AND FORCED THEM TO CONSTRUCT A ROPE MADE OUT OF THEIR OWN BEDSHEETS.

HE THEN HELD A KNIFE TO THIS FEMALE INMATE'S THROAT UNTIL GUARDS ALLOWED HIM ACCESS TO THE ROOF.
WHERE HE RAPPELLED DOWN TO THE GROUND BELOW AND MADE OFF WITH A PRISON TRUCK IN A DARING ESCAPE.
THIS JUST IN, THE POLICE HAVE RELEASED A PICTURE OF THE PERPETRATOR.
HE IS ARMED AND EXTREMELY DANGEROUS.
IF YOU SEE THIS MAN, CALL THE POLICE IMMEDIATELY.

HIS NAME IS ICHABOD JONES.
THAT'S NOT ME. I'M A BUS DRIVER, NOT A PSYCHOPATH.
HE WAS IMPRISONED FOR THE BRUTAL MURDER OF FOUR INNOCENT CIVILIANS.
NO. YOU'RE LYING. I'M NORMAL.
ON A PERSONAL NOTE, LET'S HOPE THEY CATCH AND FRY THIS LUNATIC.
I'M NORMAL. I'M NORMAL! I DON'T EVEN HEAR THE VOICE ANYMORE!
WE'LL BE RIGHT BACK WITH SPORTS.
TELL THEM I'M NORMAL!
HELP ME!
HELP ME!

BANG! BANG! BANG!

BANG!

PLEASE. I'M NOT DEAD! HELP ME!

ICHABOD JONES, YOU STAND ACCUSED ON FOUR COUNTS OF FIRST-DEGREE MURDER. HOW DO YOU PLEAD?

NOT GUILTY, YOUR HONOR, BY REASON OF CRIMINAL INSANITY.
HORSE SHIT! HOW DARE YOU!

I HOPE YOU BURN IN HELL.
I AM INNOCENT. I WAS DOING IT BECAUSE-

ENOUGH, ICHABOD.

YOU'RE ONLY MAKING IT WORSE.

YOU MADE A MISTAKE PLEADING INNOCENT.
IF WE HAD PLED GUILTY, YOU MIGHT HAVE JUST SPENT THE REST OF YOUR LIFE IN JAIL.
NOW, YOU'LL GET THE CHAIR FOR SURE IF WE CAN'T CONVINCE A JURY THAT YOU'RE CRAZY.

WHY DO YOU HATE ME SO MUCH?

SERIOUSLY? THEY FOUND YOU WITH YOUR HAND WRIST DEEP INSIDE YOUR LAST VICTIM.
YOU ARE EVERY BIT THE MONSTER THEY SAY YOU ARE.
UNFORTUNATELY, EVEN MONSTERS DESERVE A FAIR TRIAL.
POK POK

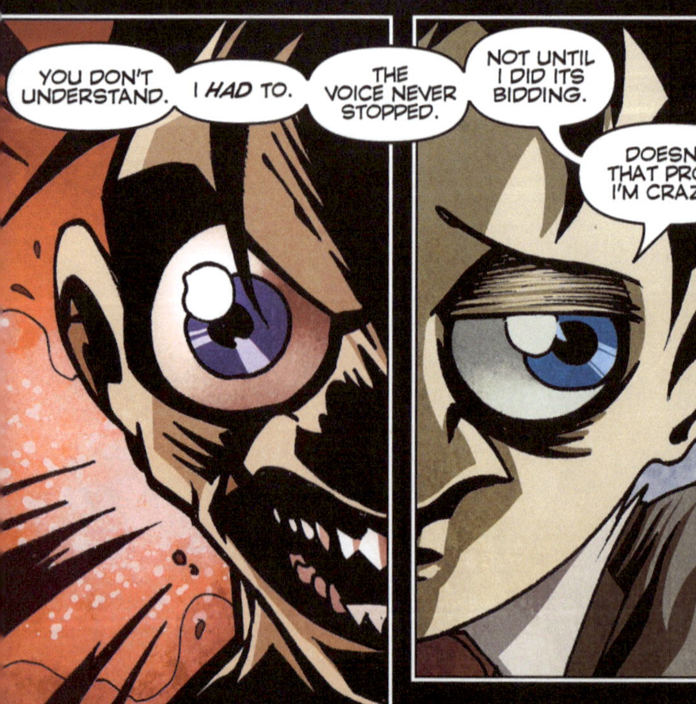

YOU DON'T UNDERSTAND.
I HAD TO.
THE VOICE NEVER STOPPED.
NOT UNTIL I DID ITS BIDDING.
DOESN'T THAT PROVE I'M CRAZY?

SAVE IT FOR THE JURY.
THEY'RE THE ONES YOU HAVE TO CONVINCE.

I'D LIKE YOU TO BELIEVE ME, TOO.

AFTER ALL, YOU ARE MY LAWYER.

I'M YOUR LAWYER, NOT YOUR FRIEND.

I'M ONLY HERE BECAUSE NOBODY ELSE WOULD TAKE YOUR CASE.
AND I AM THE LOW WOMAN ON THE TOTEM POLE.
I STILL BELIEVE IN YOU.

YOU SHOULDN'T.
I'M NOT A VERY GOOD LAWYER.

SLAM!

SLAM!
HELP!

SLAM!
HELP ME!

SLAM!
PLEASE!

PLEASE LET ME OUT.

LET ME OUT OF HERE! I'M NOT DEAD!
Calm down.

WHO SAID THAT?
It will all be okay.

I'm here to help you.
I'VE HEARD THAT BEFORE.

LOOK WHERE I ENDED UP BECAUSE OF IT.

Yes. That was... regrettable.
But I assure you,
things will be different this time.
I DON'T BELIEVE YOU.
You will.
DOUBTFUL.

There is very little air left.
If you don't listen, you won't make it to be rescued.
I DON'T WANNA!

Do you want to die?
NO.
Then calm yourself.

Take one, slow breath in.
Good.
This will all be over soon.

NOW WHAT?

Listen.

CLAP CLOP CLOP CLAP
Do you hear it?
FOOTSTEPS!

HELLO? IS SOMEONE DOWN THERE?
YES! YES! I'M DOWN HERE! HELP ME!
HANG ON. BE VERY STILL.
I'LL HAVE YOU OUT IN A JIFF.

I told you it would be okay.
LUCKY GUESS.
I don't guess.

CAN YOU HURRY UP A BIT?
QUIET! YOU'RE RUINING MY CONCENTRATION.

THRRUMP

OW. OW. OW. OW. OW.

THRRRRRRUMPA—FOOM!

AHHHHHHH.
BROOOM!

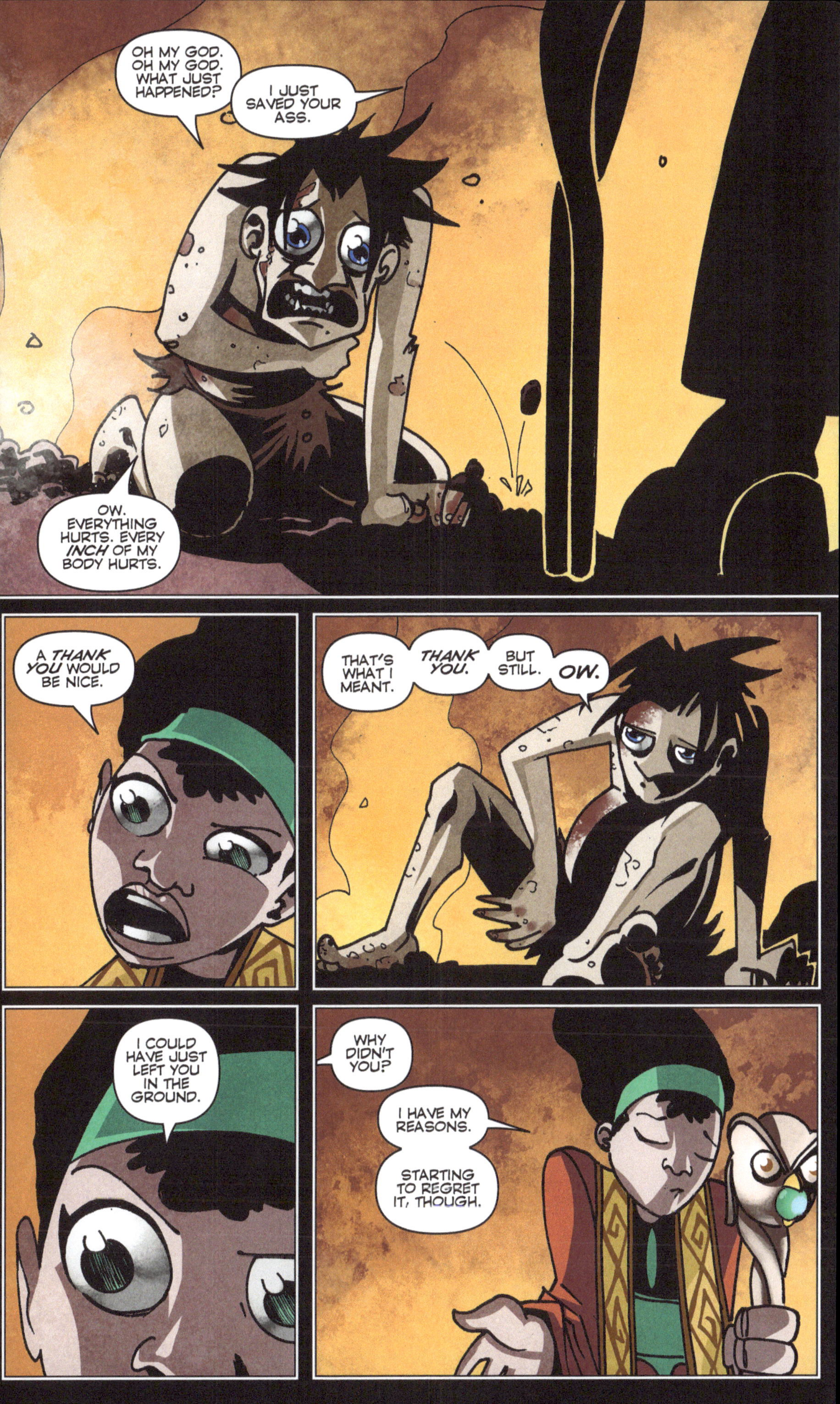

OH MY GOD. OH MY GOD. WHAT JUST HAPPENED?
I JUST SAVED YOUR ASS.
OW. EVERYTHING HURTS. EVERY *INCH* OF MY BODY HURTS.

A *THANK YOU* WOULD BE NICE.
THAT'S WHAT I MEANT.
THANK YOU.
BUT STILL.
OW.

I COULD HAVE JUST LEFT YOU IN THE GROUND.

WHY DIDN'T YOU?
I HAVE MY REASONS.
STARTING TO REGRET IT, THOUGH.

I'M SORRY. I REALLY AM GRATEFUL. THANK YOU.
THAT'S BETTER. YOU'RE WELCOME.
WHERE AM I?
THE ETERNAL DESERT. IT'S BETTER THAN A CASKET, BUT NOT BY MUCH.

FUNNY. YOU DON'T SMELL DEAD.
Sniff Sniff
I'VE BEEN TOLD THAT BEFORE.

THEN YOU'RE NOT A ZOMBIE?

NOT THAT I KNOW OF.

DAMN. I THOUGHT I WOULD AT LEAST GET SOME FRESH ZOMBIE SPLEEN OUT OF DIGGING YOU UP.
ZOMBIE SPLEEN?
IT'S A THICKENING AGENT FOR A POWERFUL HEALING PASTE, AND I'M FRESH OUT OF IT.

SO YOU WERE GONNA KILL ME?
YOU CAN'T KILL SOMETHING THAT'S ALREADY DEAD.
BUT SINCE YOU'RE NOT DEAD, I GUESS WE SHOULD GET GOING. THE DESERT IS NO PLACE FOR THE LIVING.
ESPECIALLY AFTER SUNSET.
YOU EXPECT ME TO FOLLOW YOU, AFTER YOU JUST ADMITTED WANTING TO KILL ME?
UNLESS YOU WANT TO DIE... THEN YES.

CRAMP SLURPT CHOMP NOM NOM
WHAT'S YOUR NAME, STRANGER?

ICHABOD.
Don't talk with your mouth full.
NICE TO MEET YOU, ICHABOD.
MY NAME IS MONICA FLETCHER.

BUT YOU CAN CALL ME NECROMONICA.
WIZARD OF THE APOCALYPSE.
WINK

YEAH, I'M NOT DOING THAT.

Be nice.
NO!
Ichabod!
LEAVE ME ALONE, ALRIGHT? YOU DON'T CONTROL ME.

ARE YOU TALKING TO ME?
NO.
THEN WHO ARE YOU TALKING TO?
NOBODY.
I am not nobody!
:Sigh:... THERE'S JUST THIS VOICE IN MY HEAD...

OH, IS THAT ALL?

IT WAS ENOUGH TO GET ME LOCKED AWAY IN ANOTHER LIFE.

MAYBE IT WAS CRAZY AT SOME POINT, BUT NOW IT BARELY REGISTERS.
CHOMP

ALRIGHT, I'M GOING TO BED.
YOU'RE WELCOME TO STAY HERE TONIGHT.
BUT TOMORROW YOU GOTTA GO.
I DON'T NEED ANY DEAD WEIGHT DRAGGING ME DOWN.

Thank her.
THANK YOU.

THE VOICE IN YOUR HEAD IS VERY CURIOUS, ICHABOD. VERY CURIOUS INDEED.
That's the nicest thing he's ever said about me.

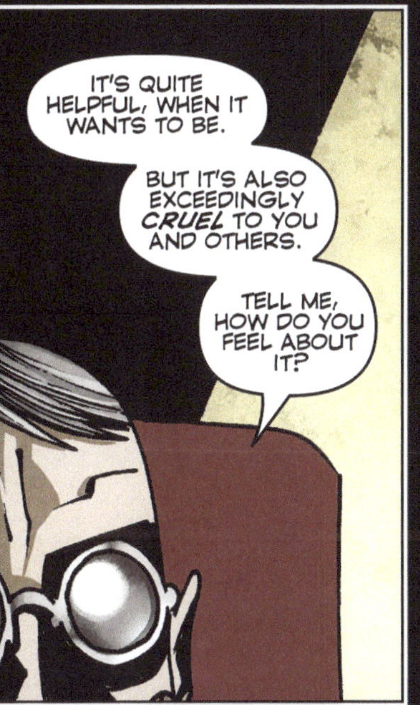

IT'S QUITE HELPFUL, WHEN IT WANTS TO BE.
BUT IT'S ALSO EXCEEDINGLY CRUEL TO YOU AND OTHERS.
TELL ME, HOW DO YOU FEEL ABOUT IT?

I HATE IT.
That, in contrast, was not very nice.
AS YOU SHOULD. IT CONVINCED YOU TO DO HORRIBLE THINGS.

AND I REGRET THEM EVERY MINUTE OF EVERY DAY.
And I regret coming to you.
I taught you to be brave. I taught you to be fearless. I taught you to hunt monsters.

you never appreciated me.
WELL, IT'S A START.

THANK YOU, DOCTOR. I DO WANT TO GET BETTER.
I BELIEVE YOU, ICHABOD.
I don't.
Not anymore.

KRIT
KRIT
KRIT
KRIT
KRIT
GRUNT

HRM?

WHA?
Ichabod! Close your eyes!

Good. Don't open them until I tell you.
Listen to my voice and trust me.

Swipe your hand across your body fast.

Brace yourself.

Block!

Bat it away!

Open your eyes, but avoid its gaze at all costs.

Grab the beast by the ears.

Now swing.
CHOF

CRAK!
Swing.

SWING!
SPLOCH!

MONICA!
That's not what she wants to be called.

I'M NOT CALLING HER THAT!
Quit being a twatwhistle.
UGH. FINE.

NECROMONICA! WAKE UP!

BUT DON'T LOOK AT THEM!

PLUOF!

NIGHTMARE ELVES!

TOK

THE WARDS MUST HAVE FAILED.
WHAT DO WE DO? WE CAN'T TAKE THEM ALL ON.

SIT LUCEAT EXPIRARE!

FUOOOOOOSHHH

THEY'RE GONE. YOU DID PRETTY WELL.
REALLY?
Yes, really. I'm very proud of you.
Why are you crying?
I JUST... DON'T HEAR THAT SOMEBODY'S PROUD OF ME VERY OFTEN.

WOAH. I DIDN'T SAY PROUD.
I AM IMPRESSED, THOUGH. I'VE NEVER SEEN ANYONE DESTROY A NIGHTMARE ELF WITH THEIR BARE HANDS.

IS THAT WHAT THOSE THINGS WERE?
THAT'S WHAT I CALL THEM.
THEY COME ON YOU IN THE NIGHT AND WHEN YOUR EYES CATCH THEIRS, THEY HYPNOTIZE YOU TO DO THEIR BIDDING.
NASTY BUGGERS...
BUT YOU HELD YOUR OWN, THOUGH.

YOU MAY BE USEFUL AFTER ALL.
THANK YOU.

THERE IS A GREAT EVIL IN THIS DESERT, ICHABOD, AND I INTEND TO RID THE WORLD OF IT.

HOW?
WITH THIS BOOK.
IT'S AN OLD TRANSCRIPTION OF ANCIENT TEXTS, BOUND IN BLOOD AND WRITTEN BY HAND HUNDREDS OF YEARS AGO.
I KNOW IT SOUNDS CRAZY, BUT SOME OF THE RUNES AND SPELLS WORK, AS YOU'VE SEEN.
TAKE A LOOK.

The Book of The Dead.
It has been lost for eons.
WILL YOU JOIN ME ON MY QUEST?
You must say yes.
Necronomicon
WHY?

Because she has the answers we seek.
The book will tell us how to end the Apocalypse.
END THE APOCALYPSE?

THAT'S THE GOAL. FIRST THIS DESERT, THEN AMERICA. AND EVENTUALLY, THE WHOLE EARTH.
ONCE WE'RE THROUGH SAVING THE WORLD, EVERYTHING CAN GO BACK TO HOW IT WAS. WON'T THAT BE AWESOME?

YEAH...

THAT'LL BE JUST SWELL.

OK, I'LL GO WITH YOU.
COOL, COOL, COOL. HAPPY YOU SAID THAT.
OTHERWISE, I WOULD'VE HAD TO KILL YOU.
WELL, I'M GLAD IT DIDN'T COME TO THAT.
ME TOO.
Me three.

KEEP UP, ICHABOD. WE DON'T HAVE ALL DAY.
IT'S SO HOT!
DO YOU DO ANYTHING EXCEPT COMPLAIN?

HOW CAN YOU...
NOT BE HOT...
AND TIRED?
YOU'RE WEARING LIKE... 100 LAYERS.

THAT'S EASY.
I'M USING A TRANSMUTATION CHARM TO KEEP COOL.
I'LL GIVE IT TO YOU, TOO, IF IT'LL QUIT YOUR BITCHING.
DEAL.

FRIGIDUS VENTUS.

AHHH.
HAPPY NOW?
VERY.
GOOD. NOW, HURRY UP.

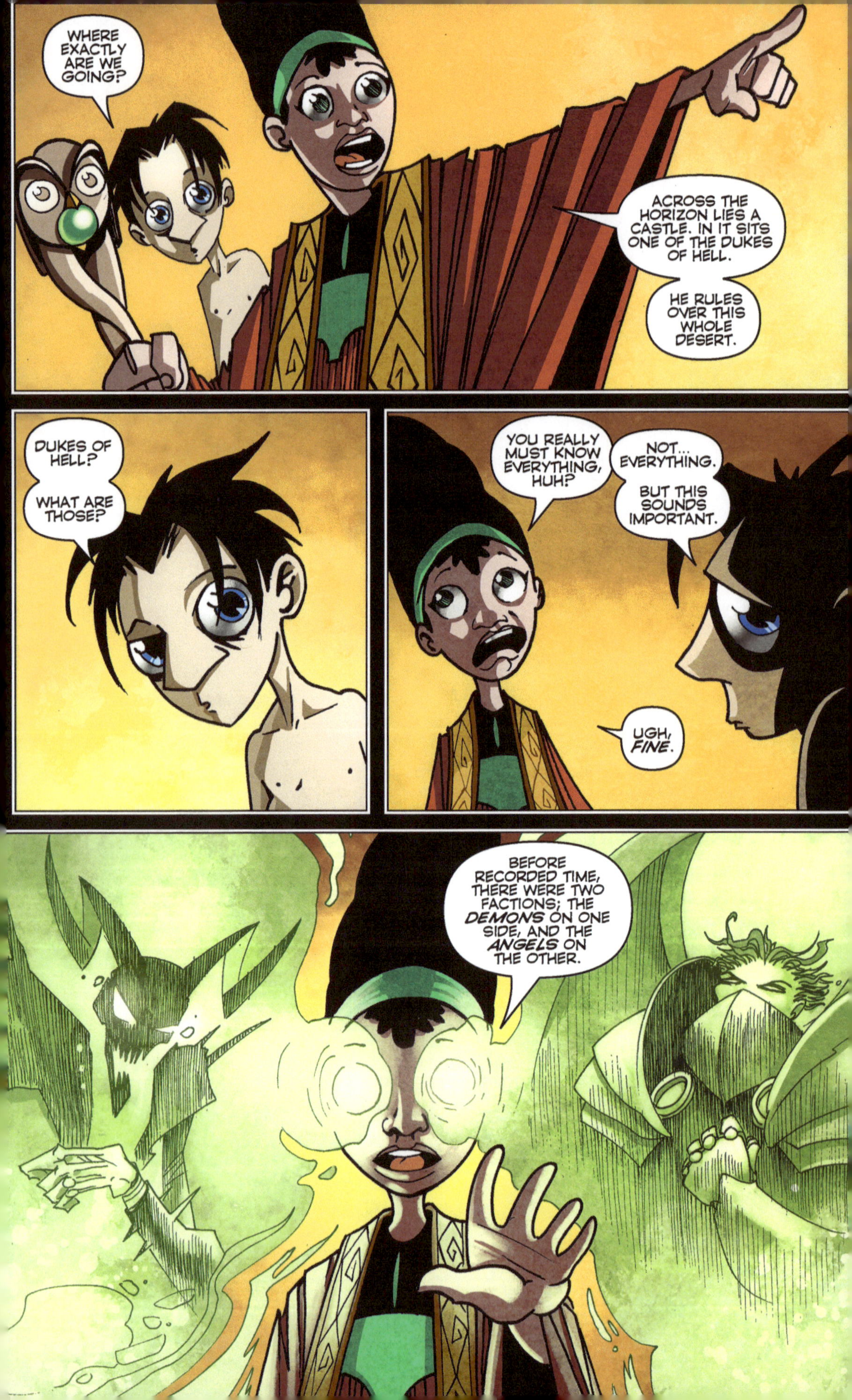

WHERE EXACTLY ARE WE GOING?
ACROSS THE HORIZON LIES A CASTLE. IN IT SITS ONE OF THE DUKES OF HELL.
HE RULES OVER THIS WHOLE DESERT.

DUKES OF HELL?
WHAT ARE THOSE?

YOU REALLY MUST KNOW EVERYTHING, HUH?
NOT... EVERYTHING.
BUT THIS SOUNDS IMPORTANT.
UGH, FINE.

BEFORE RECORDED TIME, THERE WERE TWO FACTIONS; THE DEMONS ON ONE SIDE, AND THE ANGELS ON THE OTHER.

THEY BOTH VIED FOR CONTROL OF EARTH AND HUMANITY, BUT NEITHER COULD CLAIM IT.

SO THEY CAME TO AN ACCORD.
FOR 10,000 YEARS, HUMANITY WOULD FORGE ITS OWN PATH WITHOUT INTERFERENCE FROM EITHER SIDE.
IN DOING SO, THEIR ACTIONS WOULD DECIDE WHETHER THEY BELONGED TO HEAVEN OR HELL.

AND THAT'S WHY THE APOCALYPSE HAPPENED?
YUP. THE DEMONS WON AND INVADED EARTH.
AND HERE WE ARE.
BECAUSE WE ALL SUCKED AT BEING DECENT TO EACH OTHER.
HUMANITY IS THE WORST.

I CAN'T ARGUE THERE.
BUT WHAT ABOUT THE DUKES?

I'M GETTING TO THEM.
AS THE APOCALYPSE DREW NEAR...
AND SATAN KNEW HE HAD WON...
HE APPOINTED SIX DUKES TO CARRY OUT HIS DOMINATION OF EARTH.
WHILE HE RULED OVER HELL.

AND I'M GOING TO KILL THEM ALL.
WHEN THEY'RE DEAD, I'LL TAKE DOWN SATAN, TOO...
AND THEN EVERYTHING WILL GO BACK TO NORMAL.
I like her moxie.

IT'S NOT MOXIE. IT'S STUPIDITY.
SHE'S GONNA GET HERSELF KILLED.
Not if we help her.

HOW AM I GONNA TAKE ON ONE DUKE OF HELL, LET ALONE SIX?
With my help.
YOU'RE NOTHING BUT A VOICE IN MY HEAD.
No. I am so much more.

It's time I revealed my true nature to you.
I am an angel.
So was the one that came before me.
THAT HORRIBLE VOICE WAS AN ANGEL?
Not one of our gentlest.

He's a brute engine of war. Brutal, but efficient.
HE MADE ME KILL SO MANY PEOPLE.
WHY ARE YOU IN MY HEAD? WHY WAS HE IN MY HEAD?
We tried so hard, for so long, to save humanity.

But eventually, we knew that all hope was lost.
All we could do was prepare the chosen to fight against the darkness.
Any way we could.
CHOSEN?
Chosen to help stop the Apocalypse.

But every one of them is dead.
Every one.
Except you.
CAN WE GO NOW?

UMMM, YEAH...SURE. JUST GIVE ME JUST A SEC--

UUUUGH.

POF

Get up, you pussy!

I...CAN'T.

We don't have time for this!

Take the knife and open her up.

WHY?

So we can find the evil that poisoned her soul.

WHAT AM I DOING?
Cut her chest to naval.
THAT'S DISGUSTING.
Do it.

Good.
Now, search for a hard, metallic, black ball.
FRUGGG

THAT'S CRAZY.
You just killed a woman because a voice told you to do it.
I don't think you can judge crazy anymore.
FAIR ENOUGH.

WHAT IS THIS?
That is pure, concentrated evil.
It is infecting many people on this planet.
And you have to stop it before it's too late.

HOW?
You aren't going to like it.
GULP
You're going to have to kill a lot of people.

GET UP!

I'M UP.
AT LEAST I THINK I'M UP.

I KNEW IT WAS A MISTAKE TO BRING YOU WITH ME.
I SHOULD JUST LEAVE YOU HERE TO DIE.
BUT I WON'T.

EVEN THOUGH I WANT TO.
THANK YOU.
DAMN RIGHT THANK YOU.

EVERY MINUTE WE WASTE IS ANOTHER MINUTE EVIL TIGHTENS ITS STRANGLEHOLD ON THIS PLANET.
AND YOU'RE DOING NOTHING BUT SLOWING ME DOWN.

I'M NOT TRYING TO BE A BURDEN.
WELL, YOU ARE FAILING MISERABLY AT IT.

THAT SOUNDS LIKE ME.
Keep your chin up.

OH PLEASE. I WILL NOT HAVE YOU WEEPING YOUR SAD STORY TO ME.
WE ALL HAVE SAD STORIES.

RRRRRRRRRRRRRRR
I WAS A TENURED PROFESSOR OF ARCHAEOLOGY AT STANFORD.
NOW, I AM A WIZARD IN THE APOCALYPSE.
MY NEW LIFE SUCKS, BUT IT IS WHAT IT IS.
WE ALL HAVE OUR BURDENS.
WHAT IS THAT?
OH NO.

QUICK! GET BEHIND ME!
BRRRRRRRRRRRR
MURUM EXSTRUERE!
FRRRROOOOOMMM
COME ON! THAT WON'T SLOW THEM DOWN MUCH.

OR, MAYBE IT WON'T SLOW THEM AT ALL.
WHERE ARE WE GOING?
I DON'T KNOW.
KRAAAAMM

THERE! AN OASIS!

THAT'S JUST AN ILLUSION OF YOUR MIND.

THEN HOW COME YOU CAN SEE IT, TOO?
GOOD POINT.

THEY'RE GAINING ON US.
WE CAN GAIN SOME DISTANCE IF WE ROLL DOWN THE HILL!

Tuck your head tightly into your body!

BARF! BARF!
BARF!
BARF!
WHAT?
WHERE AM I?
WHAT'S GOING ON?
ARE THOSE DOGS?

HELLO?
VOICE?
ARE YOU THERE?

GREAT. THIS IS THE LITERALLY WORST TIME TO ABANDON ME.
I GUESS I HAVE TO FIGURE THIS OUT ON MY OWN.

BARF! BARF!
BARF!
THOSE DOGS DO NOT LOOK FRIENDLY.

SPLOOSH!

>GASP<
GET BACK!

TEMPESTAS HARENAE!
HUH?
OH. I'M BACK HERE NOW.
GREAT, I GUESS.

FWWOOOOOOOSSHHH

GOOD. YOU'RE NOT DEAD.
IS THAT A PLUS?
NEBULOUS.

COME ON. THEY'LL BE BACK, AND IN GREATER NUMBERS.
WHAT JUST HAPPENED?

WEREN'T WE JUST IN THE WOODS?
I'M NOT GOING TO ANSWER THAT BECAUSE IT'S STUPID.
THAT'S A NO, THEN?
I SEE.
We never left the desert.

JUST BE CAREFUL. DON'T TOUCH ANYTHING.
WATER!

WHAT DID I SAY?
She's probably right.

I DON'T CARE. I'M SO THIRSTY.
It could be toxic.
THEN I'LL DIE.
FRANKLY, DEATH MIGHT BE PREFERABLE AT THIS POINT.
Don't say things like that.

WHY? IT'S THE TRU--
I-I-I-ICHABOD?

OH MY GOD.

CATHY!
YOU!
I NEVER THOUGHT I WOULD SEE YOU AGAIN.
YOU!

SHUT UP!

WAIT, YOU HEARD THAT?

YES.
EVER SINCE YOU DIED.

I DIDN'T DIE.
YOU'RE RIGHT, OBVIOUSLY.
EVER SINCE YOU DIDN'T DIE, BUT WE THOUGHT YOU DIED, I HAVE BEEN HEARING A VOICE.
I THINK IT'S YOUR VOICE. THE ONE YOU HEARD.

Don't listen to it!
Don't tell them what to do!
SHUT UP!

That's it! Come to the mortal plane and face me.

That would be unwise.
I don't care!
AHHH!

WHAT IS HAPPENING HERE?
Fine, it will be my great pleasure to destroy you in the flesh.
Big words for so weak a being!

UUUUH...

SERIOUSLY,
WHAT IS GOING
ON HERE?

YOU'RE BREAKING THE RULES, URIEL!
WHAT RULES, SAMAEL?
IN CASE YOU HAVEN'T NOTICED, THERE ARE NO RULES ANYMORE. THE DEVIL WON SOME TIME AGO.

WE'RE STILL NOT SUPPOSED TO BE SEEN BY HUMANS!
WHO CARES!? WE ALREADY FAILED!
GOD CARES. THAT'S WHO!

THE SAME GOD THAT STOOD BY AND LET THIS HAPPEN?

YEAH. THAT ONE. HE'S AN IDIOT, BUT HE'S STILL OUR BOSS!

CAN ONE OF YOU PLEASE EXPLAIN TO ME WHAT'S GOING ON?

THIS IS NOT GOOD, ICHABOD. NOT GOOD AT ALL.
WHY NOT, DOCTOR BUTLER?

DON'T YOU SEE? THE TWO SIDES OF YOUR PSYCHOSIS ARE MANIFESTING THEMSELVES IN CORPOREAL FORM, FIGHTING FOR YOUR VERY SOUL...
I THOUGHT WE WERE BEYOND THIS. I'M AFRAID THIS IS VERY BAD.

GUARD. PLEASE BRING ICHABOD FOR ANOTHER PROCEDURE.
TUP

NO, PLEASE.
I REALLY HAVE SUCH HIGH HOPES FOR YOU.

THAT IS WHY IT'S SO UPSETTING WHEN YOU DISAPPOINT ME.

GO EASY ON HIM TODAY.
YES, DOCTOR.
BUT NOT TOO EASY.
YOU GOT IT.

TZZ-TZZ

TRRTZ
BRRRTZZ

OW.
MY HEAD.

ARE YOU OKAY?
NO. I DON'T EVEN KNOW WHAT THAT MEANS ANYMORE.

I SHOULD LOP OFF YOUR HEAD.
TRY IT.

HEY! I'M SICK OF ASKING NICELY.
SOMEBODY EXPLAIN WHAT'S GOING ON RIGHT NOW OR I'M GOING TO--
WELL, I DON'T KNOW WHAT I'M GONNA DO, BECAUSE THIS IS SOME CRAZY ASS SHIT.
BUT IT WILL BE BAD.
SO, START EXPLAINING.

GLADLY.
IF YOU INSIST.

I'M GLAD YOU'RE OKAY, CATHY.
SAME.

IT'S SO GOOD TO SEE YOU, ICHABOD.

WHAT HAPPENED TO THE OTHERS?

OH, ICHABOD, IT WAS HORRIBLE. I TRIED TO SAVE THEM...
I TRIED TO BE LIKE YOU...
BUT...

I COULDN'T PROTECT THEM.
THEY'RE ALL DEAD.
EVERY SINGLE ONE.
IT'S OKAY.
NO. IT'S NOT.

YOU DID YOUR BEST.

I KNOW.
AND IT WASN'T GOOD ENOUGH.
THAT'S THE WORST PART.

THIS IS YOURS. I DON'T DESERVE IT.

SURE YOU DO.
DON'T PATRONIZE ME.
NOT YOU.

THANK YOU FOR KEEPING IT SAFE.

THAT'S ABOUT ALL I COULD PROTECT.
ONE STUPID KNIFE.
I STILL APPRECIATE IT.
COME ON. LET'S JOIN THE OTHERS.

SO, LET ME GET THIS STRAIGHT.
YOU ARE ANGELS.
CORRECT.

ICHABOD WAS CHOSEN TO HELP END THE APOCALYPSE.
ALONG WITH A BUNCH OF OTHER PEOPLE.

YES, BUT EVERYBODY ELSE WHO WAS CHOSEN IS DEAD.
AND NOW WE'RE ON OUR OWN.

US AGAINST ABOUT A MILLION DEMONS.
THAT SOUND ABOUT RIGHT?

YUP. THAT'S SPOT ON.
YOU NAILED IT.

WELL, THAT IS SOME BUUUUULLSHIT.

I AGREE WITH HER.

ME THREE.

YOU'RE RIGHT. IT'S NOT GREAT, BUT THERE IS GOOD NEWS.

IS THERE?
WELL, I'D LOVE TO HEAR WHAT YOU CONSIDER GOOD NEWS IN ALL OF THIS.

WE CAN STILL END THE APOCALYPSE.

HOW?

UMMM...

WE.
DON'T... KNOW.

WHAT DO YOU MEAN YOU DON'T KNOW?

THIS IS EMBARRASSING.
WE WROTE IT DOWN SOMEWHERE... AND THEN...

WE LOST IT, OKAY?

WHAT DO YOU MEAN YOU LOST IT?

WE HAD A COPY OF THE AGREEMENT.
HELL HAD A COPY OF OUR AGREEMENT.
AND WE...LOST OURS.
GOD HAS NO IDEA WHERE HE PUT IT.

I DON'T UNDERSTAND. I THOUGHT GOD WAS ALL KNOWING.

THAT. IS A LIE.
NOT A LIE, REALLY.
WE JUST... BEEFED UP HIS STATS A BIT.
IT'S MORE LIKE HE TRIES REALLY HARD.
NOT THAT HARD.

AND YET. THIS HAPPENED.
PROVING HE IS NOT ALL POWERFUL, EITHER.
ANOTHER STAT WE JUICED A BIT.
"WE" IS A MISLEADING WORD.
THE METATRON WORKED ALONE ON THE WHOLE FLAWLESS GOD MYTHOLOGY... FOR THE MOST PART.

THEN HOW ARE WE GOING TO FIGURE OUT HOW TO END THIS APOCALYPSE?

THE BOOK YOU HAVE. THE NECRONOMICON. IT HAS HELL'S COPY OF OUR AGREEMENT.
THE ANSWER IS IN THAT BOOK.

SO THEY LOST THEIR COPY, TOO?
IT WOULD APPEAR SO, IN A MANNER OF SPEAKING.

MAY I SEE IT?

FINE.
DON'T LOSE MY PLACE.

A BUNCH OF THESE PAGES ARE MISSING?

DID YOU KNOW A BUNCH OF THESE PAGES ARE MISSING?
YEAH. I HAVE EYES, DON'T I?

BUT THE REST OF THE BOOK WORKED ALRIGHT, SO I DIDN'T WORRY ABOUT IT.
BESIDES, I HADN'T GOTTEN THAT FAR YET.

THE ANSWER WAS IN THOSE PAGES.
WE MUST FIND THEM.

I DON'T KNOW WHAT TO TELL YOU.
MAYBE TALK TO YOUR ALL-KNOWING, NOT ALL-KNOWING GOD ABOUT WHERE THEY ARE.

OH WAIT, YOU CAN'T.
BECAUSE HE'S A FRAUD.
STOMP!

WHAT WAS THAT?

STOMP!
UHHHHHHH...

RRRAAAAAA!
NOT GOOD.
STOMP!

AN INFERINI.
IT CAN'T BE. THEY'RE SUPPOSED TO BE EXTINCT.
WELL THEY CLEARLY AREN'T.
ARE YOU GOING TO MARVEL AT IT, OR KILL IT?
RIGHT. STAY HERE.
LIKE THE GOOD OLD DAYS.
ON THREE.
ONE.
TWO.
THR--

TUFF

FRAAAM!

NEW PLAN.
NEW PLAN!

DO SOMETHING!
ME DO SOMETHING?
YOU'RE THE CHOSEN ONE!

THE BOOK.
WHAT DOES THE BOOK SAY ABOUT THOSE THINGS?
IT MUST SAY SOMETHING.

RIGHT. WHAT DID THEY CALL IT AGAIN?
INFERIOR?
INFERINI.

HERE IT IS.
INFERINI.
RRAAA!
PLEASE HURRY.
I'M TRYING!
INFERINI ARE TRACKING DEMONS.
THEY WILL NEVER STOP UNTIL THEY CAPTURE THEIR PREY AND BRING IT TO THEIR MASTER.

SO IT'S HUNTING SOMETHING?
SEEMS LIKE IT.
WHAT IS IT AFTER?
COULD BE ANYTHING, OR ANYBODY.
BUT IF I HAD TO GUESS...
ONE, OR ALL, OF US.

NO!
THEY ARE NOT TAKING US.

DO THAT COOLING SPELL ON IT!
THAT'S NOT GONNA WORK!
JUST TRY IT!

FRIGIDUS VENTUS.
FWOOSHH

UH OH.
TWONK

BRAAAM!

DO SOMETHING ELSE!
I'M TRYING!
HERE YOU GO. THIS MIGHT WORK, BUT IT'S VERY ADVANCED. I DON'T KNOW IF I CAN--
JUST DO IT!

ET DAEMONIUM AB INFERNO, ET CONTROL TIBI!

IT'S A BINDING SPELL.

IT'S WORKING!
I CAN'T HOLD IT FOR LONG.

YOU DON'T HAVE TO.

FOR THE GLORY OF HEAVEN!

TRUOKK

FRRAAAA!

TRAAKK

RRUUMMBLE

YOU DID WELL.
FOR HUMANS.

DID BETTER THAN YOU.

WELL, THE MONSTER IS TECHNICALLY DEAD BECAUSE OF ME, SO...
NO.
BUT YOU DID WELL AND FOUGHT VALIANTLY, ALL OF YOU.

WHY DID WE HAVE TO FIGHT AT ALL?
WHAT WAS IT COMING FOR AND WHO SENT IT?

MOST LIKELY BEELZEBUB, THE LORD OF FLIES.
HE IS THE ONLY ONE WHO COULD SUMMON SUCH A BEAST.
HE CONTROLS THIS DESERT.

HE PROBABLY KNOWS SOMETHING ABOUT THE MISSING PAGES IN THE NECRONOMICON, TOO.

HE WON'T HELP US.

NO. HE WON'T.
THAT'S WHY WE MUST MAKE HIM SUFFER UNTIL HE TELLS US WHAT WE NEED TO KNOW.

YOU'RE TALKING ABOUT STARTING WAR WITH HELL.

IF WE'RE GOING TO STOP THIS APOCALYPSE, THEN WE CAN'T BE SCARED TO GET OUR HANDS DIRTY.

YOU TAUGHT ME THAT.
I'M SURPRISED YOU LISTENED.

VERY WELL.
IF YOU ARE ALL IN AGREEMENT, I HAVE NO PROBLEM ANTAGONIZING THE DARK LORD.

I DO. YOU DON'T KNOW WHAT KIND OF HELLFIRE HE COULD UNLEASH ON US.
I'M AWARE OF IT.
WE SHOULD DO IT ANYWAY.

AGREED.
THIS APOCALYPSE NEEDS TO END.
IF THIS WILL HELP, THEN I'M IN.

JUST SO WE'RE CLEAR. I DON'T KNOW IF THIS WILL HELP OR HURT.

THAT DOESN'T SOUND LIKE A GREAT PLAN, BUT IT'S BETTER THAN NOTHING.
IS IT THOUGH?
IT'S ALL WE HAVE, CHOSEN ONE.

ARE YOU SURE YOU'RE READY FOR THIS?
FIGHTING DEMONS IS NOT THE SAME AS KILLING INFECTED PEOPLE.

I'M NOT READY FOR ANY OF THIS. NONE OF US ARE.

BUT WE HAVE TO TRY.

I'VE BEEN READY FOR THIS FIGHT FOR A LONG TIME.
AGREED.

ALRIGHT THEN. LET'S DO IT.
ANGELS CAN'T TECHNICALLY DIE.
BUT YES.
WE'RE GONNA DIE, RIGHT?
WONDERFUL.

ICHABOD JONES.
YOU HAVE BEEN FOUND NOT GUILTY BY REASON OF CRIMINAL INSANITY.

YOU WILL BE REMANDED INTO THE CUSTODY OF THE STATE PSYCHIATRIC WARD UNTIL SUCH TIME AS THEY DEEM THAT YOU ARE NOT A DANGER TO YOURSELF OR OTHERS.

BEFORE I RELEASE YOU, I FEEL IT IS INCUMBENT ON ME TO EXPRESS THAT IN MY TWENTY YEARS ON THE BENCH, I HAVE NEVER SEEN A MORE VILE OR DESPICABLE EXCUSE FOR A HUMAN.

IF IT WERE UP TO ME, I WOULD SEE YOU FRY AND SMILE WHILE YOU BURNED.

HOWEVER, YOUR PEERS HAVE SPOKEN. MAY GOD HAVE MERCY ON YOUR SOUL.

BAM!

THANK YOU.
DON'T THANK ME.

I WAS JUST DOING MY JOB.

FRANKLY, I AGREE WITH THE JUDGE.
EXCEPT FOR ONE THING.

WHAT'S THAT?

I HOPE GOD TAKES NO MERCY ON YOUR SOUL.

I DON'T KNOW IF I CAN DO THIS.
YOU CAN DO IT.
MAYBE, BUT BINDING HUNDREDS OF DEMONS AT ONCE?

WHAT IF I DON'T HAVE ENOUGH POWER?

YOU WON'T BE ALONE.
YOU WILL USE MY ENERGY TO EXPAND YOUR OWN.

I'VE NEVER USED SOMEONE'S ENERGY BEFORE, EITHER.
THIS IS SO STUPID.

IT WILL BE OKAY. YOU'LL BE GREAT.
YEAH. WE BELIEVE IN YOU.

THAT'S EVEN WORSE.
IF I FAIL, YOU'LL ALL BE DEAD.

I'M OKAY WITH THAT.
COULDN'T BE ANY WORSE THAN THIS.

BESIDES, YOU'RE NOT GOING TO FAIL, OKAY?

OKAY, I GUESS.

IT'S NOT LIKE WE HAVE ANOTHER CHOICE.
NOT UNLESS YOU CHICKEN OUT.

NO.
WE'RE DOING THIS.
NOBODY IS CHICKENING OUT TODAY.

I DID TRAIN YOU WELL, DIDN'T I?
NOPE. YOU WERE A PSYCHOPATH AND TURNED ME INTO A MONSTER.
BUT LOOK AT YOU NOW.

GIVE ME YOUR KNIFE.

WHY?
IT'S BROKEN IN HALF.

SO I MAY MEND AND BLESS IT.

YOU CAN DO THAT?
OF COURSE. I'M AN ANGEL. I AM LITERALLY HOLINESS INCARNATE.

IN NOMINE PATRIS ET FILII ET SPIRITUS SANCTI.

THERE. NOW THIS KNIFE WILL BE ABLE TO KILL THE DARK PRINCE BEELZEBUB.

WE'RE HERE TO *CAPTURE* BEELZEBUB, NOT KILL HIM.
IDEALLY.
BUT THE BEST LAID PLANS...
AND IF ICHABOD NEEDS TO ATTACK, NOW AT LEAST HE HAS A WEAPON.

I'M NOT SURE HOW LONG I CAN HOLD THEM ONCE THE SPELL STARTS, SO DON'T DAWDLE.

PROMISE ME YOU'LL STAY HERE NO MATTER WHAT.
I PROMISE.
NO MATTER WHAT.
NO MATTER WHAT.

GOOD.
LET'S GET STARTED, THEN.

ET DAEMONIUM AB INFERNO, ET CONTROL TIBI.
ET DAEMONIUM AB INFERNO, ET CONTROL TIBI.
ET DAEMONIUM AB INFERNO, ET CONTROL TIBI.

IT'S WORKING.
FOR NOW.

YOU REALLY HAVE BECOME A FINE WARRIOR, ICHABOD.
I KNOW I WAS HARD ON YOU, BUT IT MADE YOU TOUGH.
IT DROVE ME CRAZY.
LITERALLY.

BE THAT AS IT MAY, MY TRAINING BROUGHT YOU HERE NOW.
YOU COULD HAVE BEEN NICER.
OR TOLD ME THE TRUTH.

I WOULD HAVE UNDERSTOOD.

I TOLD YOU WHAT YOU NEEDED TO KNOW.
SKREECH

WHAT WAS THAT?

IT'S ALWAYS SOMETHING, ISN'T IT?
UNFORTUNATELY.
SKREEECH!

THEY'RE NOT SAFE.

AND THEY CAN'T MAINTAIN THEIR CONCENTRATION IN THIS BEDLAM.
FWOOSH!

GO!
YOU'LL HAVE TO CAPTURE HIM ON YOUR OWN.
BUT WHAT ABOUT BEELZEBUB?

HOW?

FIGURE IT OUT!
AND HURRY.
I CAN'T FIGHT THIS BEAST OFF FOR LONG.
FWOOOSH!

UGH. LORD OF FLIES IS RIGHT.
THIS PLACE IS DISGUSTING.

ICHABOD?
CATHY?
WHAT ARE YOU DOING HERE?
YOU PROMISED NOT TO MOVE FOR ANY REASON.

I KNOW.
IT'S JUST THAT...
THERE WAS THIS DRAGON BREATHING FIRE ON US.
AND I DIDN'T WANT TO GET BURNED ALIVE.

SO, YOU'D RATHER BE RIPPED APART BY DEMONS?
OBVIOUSLY, YES. WOULDN'T ANYBODY?
LET'S NOT DIE, THOUGH, IF WE CAN HELP IT.
JUST STAY CLOSE.

ADIURO TE FUGERE DAEMONIUM.
ADIURO TE FUGERE DAEMONIUM.
ADIURO TE FUGERE DAEMONIUM.
WHAT ARE YOU MUMBLING?

IT'S A SPELL TO HELP US CAPTURE BEELZEBUB.
I HOPE WE WON'T NEED IT.

IT'S SO CONFUSING.
I THINK I'M GETTING A MIGRAINE LOOKING AT IT.
JUST KEEP PRACTICING.
WE'LL BE FINE.

BZZZ BZZ BZZZZ
WELL, WELL, WELL.
VISITORS.
I HAVEN'T EATEN IN SO LONG.
WHO'S THERE?
S-S-SHOW YOURSELF.

ARE YOU SURE YOU WANT THAT?
MOST WHO LOOK UPON MY TRUE VISAGE GO MAD.
≥GULP≤
Y-Y-YES.
DO YOUR WORST!
VERY WELL.
IF YOU INSIST.
BZZZ BZZ BZZ BZZZZZBZZZZBZZZZ

BZZZBZZBZZZZBZZZZZZBZZZ
VERY SMART TO USE A BINDING SPELL ON MY GUARDS.
THEY ARE LOYAL, BUT DUMB AS ROCKS.

I WILL NOT BE SO EASILY CONTROLLED.
MY GOD, YOU'RE HIDEOUS.
THANK YOU.

ADIURA ME FINGERE DIAMOND!
WAIT, THAT'S NOT RIGHT.
ADIURO TE FUGERE DAEMONI--

ENOUGH OF YOUR PRATTLE.
SOK!

CATHY!
TUFF

YOU'LL PAY FOR THAT.
UNLIKELY.

URIEL!
I CAN'T HOLD IT BACK ANY LONGER!

HRM?
SAMAEL!

BE GONE, FOUL BEAST!

FRAAAAKK

OH NO.
THEY'RE WAKING UP.

WE NEED A NEW PLAN.

DELICIOUS.

YOUR FELLOWSHIP HAS FAILED.
AND NOW, THEY HAVE LEFT YOU ALONE.
WITH ME.

DON'T TOUCH HIM!
YOU CAN HAVE THE CARCASS ONCE I AM DONE WITH HIS SOUL.

WHAT IS THIS?
SO YOU DO HAVE IT.

THE BOOK OF THE DEAD.
WE HAVE BEEN LOOKING FOR THIS EVERYWHERE.

HOW GLORIOUS.
NOW, I WILL RETURN THE DARK LORD'S MOST PRECIOUS PRIZE.
AND DELIVER HIM YOUR ETERNAL SOULS.
NO, YOU WON'T!!!

FOOLISH.
FRRAAZZZ

YOU HAVE A FIERY SOUL.
SWIIISHH!

BZZZ BZZ
AND NOW...

BZZZZZZZZZZZ
IT BELONGS TO ME!
STOMP!

NOT TODAY, DEMON.

ADIURO TE FUGERE DAEMONIUM. ADIURO TE FUGERE DAEMONIUM. ADIURO TE FUGERE DAEMONIUM.

GET OFF ME!
IT'S WORKING!

WHERE ARE THE RIPPED FINAL PAGES OF THE NECRONOMICON?
I WILL NEVER REVEAL ANYTHING TO YOU, FOUL HUMAN.

HOW DO WE END THE APOCALYPSE?!?
TELL ME BEFORE I LOSE MY PATIENCE!

HAHAHAHAHAHAHA!
WHAT'S SO FUNNY?
YOU.
AND THE REST OF YOUR KIND.
PITIFUL.

YOU HUMANS THINK YOU ARE SO SUPERIOR.
SO GOOD.
SO PURE.

BUT I SMELL THE BLOODLUST OOZING OFF YOU.

GOD GAVE HUMANITY TEN THOUSAND YEARS TO PROVE YOUR WORTH.
AND YOU FAILED.
BECAUSE YOU ARE PURE EVIL.

WE DID YOU A FAVOR TAKING OVER THE WORLD.
BEFORE YOU DESTROYED IT.

I CANNOT WAIT TO PULL THE BONES FROM YOUR FLESH FOR THE REST OF ETERNITY.

WE ARE NOTHING LIKE YOU.
AND WE'RE GOING TO PROVE IT.

UNFORTUNATELY, YOU'LL BE TOO DEAD TO SEE IT.
ICHABOD. KILL HIM.

WAIT!
UMMM...

THIS ISN'T THE WAY.
IF YOU DESTROY HIM, YOU'LL BRING THE WRATH OF HELL UPON US ALL!

WE CAN STILL CAPTURE HIM AND ESCAPE THIS PLACE.
THAT WAS THE PLAN.

PLANS CHANGE.
I CAN'T HOLD HIM MUCH LONGER, ICHABOD.
YOU PROMISED TO HELP ME END THIS EVIL.

SO END IT!

CATHY!
LOOK WHAT HE IS CAPABLE OF.
HE WILL NEVER HELP US.

YOU MUST DESTROY HIM!

IT IS YOUR CHOICE, MONSTER HUNTER.
BUT MAKE IT QUICKLY.

WE CAN'T RISK HIS EVIL SPREADING.
I'M SORRY.

NO!

FRRRAAAAAZZ

FWOOOOOMM!

WHAT HAVE YOU DONE?
WHAT WE HAD TO DO.
NO.
YOU HAVE DOOMED US ALL.

ARE YOU OKAY?
I THINK SO.
DID WE WIN?
I THINK SO.

WOULD YOU LOOK AT THAT?
WE REALLY CAN SAVE THE WORLD.

YES, BUT AT WHAT COST?
ANY COST IS WORTH IT IF WE CAN END THIS APOCALYPSE.

WHAT ABOUT THE COST OF YOUR IMMORTAL SOUL?
I SAID ANY COST.
AND I MEANT IT.

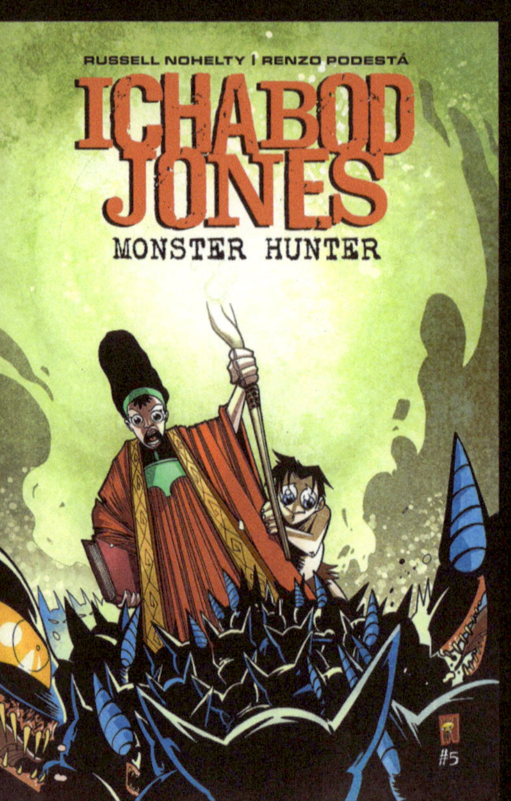

RUSSELL NOHELTY | RENZO PODESTÁ
ICHABOD JONES
MONSTER HUNTER
#5

RUSSELL NOHELTY | RENZO PODESTÁ
OPTION A
ICHABOD JONES
WELCOME TO MY NIGHTMARE

RUSSELL NOHELTY | RENZO PODESTÁ
OPTION C
ICHABOD JONES
WELCOME TO MY NIGHTMARE

RUSSELL NOHELTY | RENZO PODESTÁ
OPTION D
ICHABOD JONES
WELCOME TO MY NIGHTMARE

RUSSELL NOHELTY | RENZO PODESTÁ
ICHABOD JONES
MONSTER HUNTER
Opt. C

RUSSELL NOHELTY | RENZO PODESTÁ
ICHABOD JONES
MONSTER HUNTER
Opt. A

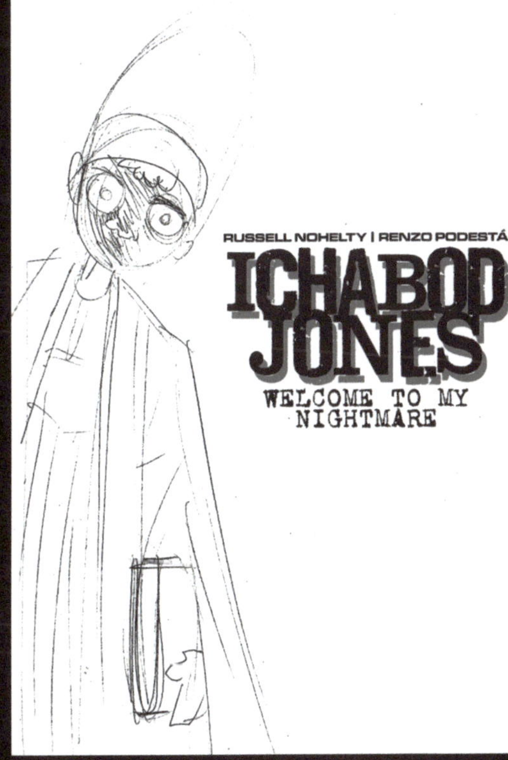

RUSSELL NOHELTY | RENZO PODESTÁ
ICHABOD JONES
WELCOME TO MY NIGHTMARE

RUSSELL NOHELTY | RENZO PODESTÁ
ICHABOD JONES
MONSTER HUNTER

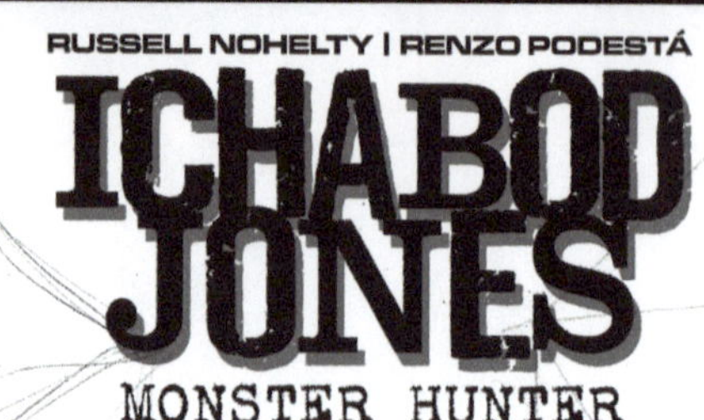

RUSSELL NOHELTY | RENZO PODESTÁ
ICHABOD JONES
MONSTER HUNTER

Opt. A

RUSSELL NOHELTY | RENZO PODESTÁ
ICHABOD JONES
MONSTER HUNTER
Opt. B

RUSSELL NOHELTY | RENZO PODESTÁ
ICHABOD JONES
MONSTER HUNTER
Opt. C

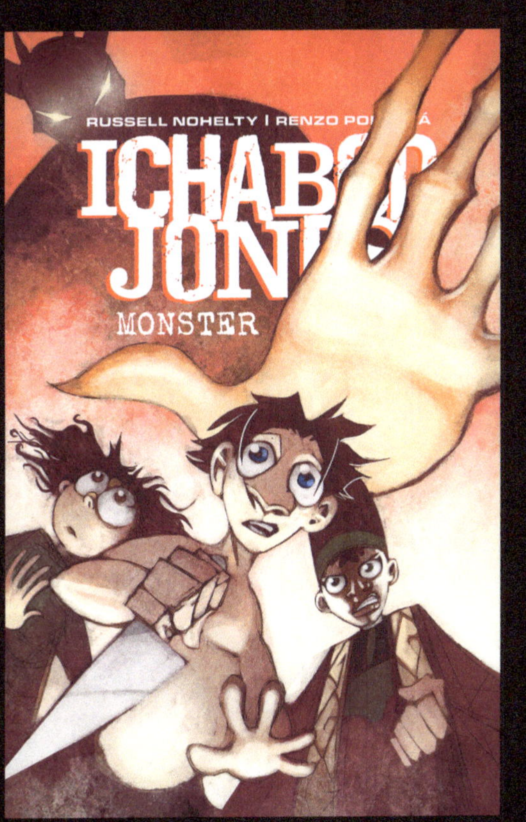

RUSSELL NOHELTY | RENZO PODESTÁ
ICHABOD JONES
MONSTER

RUSSELL NOHELTY | RENZO PODESTÁ
ICHABOD JONES
MONSTER HUNTER
Opt. A

RUSSELL NOHELTY | RENZO PODESTÁ
ICHABOD JONES
MONSTER HUNTER
Opt. B

RUSSELL NOHELTY | RENZO PODESTÁ
ICHABOD JONES
MONSTER HUNTER
Opt. C

www.ingramcontent.com/pod-product-compliance
Lightning Source LLC
Chambersburg PA
CBHW041925180726
48295CB00003B/80